Pickles
the
Mermaid

Written by
Laura Strachan

Illustrated by
Michelle Simpson

Published by Miriam Laundry Publishing Company
miriamlaundry.com

HC ISBN 978-1-77944-102-7
PB ISBN 978-1-77944-101-0
e-Book ISBN 978-1-77944-100-3

FIRST EDITION

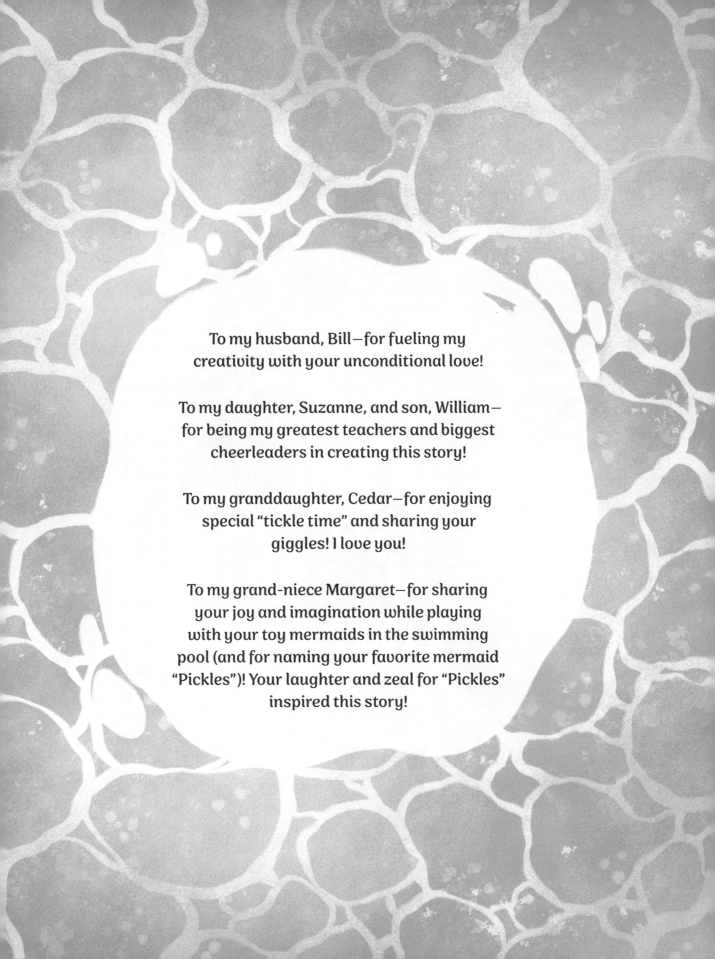

To my husband, Bill—for fueling my creativity with your unconditional love!

To my daughter, Suzanne, and son, William—for being my greatest teachers and biggest cheerleaders in creating this story!

To my granddaughter, Cedar—for enjoying special "tickle time" and sharing your giggles! I love you!

To my grand-niece Margaret—for sharing your joy and imagination while playing with your toy mermaids in the swimming pool (and for naming your favorite mermaid "Pickles")! Your laughter and zeal for "Pickles" inspired this story!

Deep beneath the sea's shimmering surface, past the thick kelp forest and way beyond the bustling coral gardens, there lived a mermaid named Pickles.

Yes—Pickles! *Why Pickles, you ask?*

Because Pickles eats pickles morning, noon and night.

Pickles are crunchy, salty, sweet, sour, bumpy and green.
Eating them makes Pickles giggle and feel silly!

Whenever her sea friends swim near, Pickles asks,
"Would you like a tickle or a pickle?" They always want both!

Giggles echo in the water around her.

But there is one mermaid who doesn't like Pickles.
Rainy laughs and makes fun of her.
"Pickles? What kind of name is that? Haha!"

One of Pickles' friends tries to console her,
"Rainy is just jealous!"

Pickles tries to avoid Rainy and hides when she sees her coming. But Rainy lurks around like a dark cloud and finds Pickles. *"Ha!"* Rainy sneers,

"You look like a pickle *AND* smell stinky like one too! *YUCK!*"

Pickles cries every time. Then, one day, she swims and swims until she's far, far away.

She sees a murky cave and goes inside to hide.
Rainy won't find me here, Pickles thinks,
hugging herself and whimpering.

Suddenly, she notices glow worms lighting up the cave.

Bubbles emerge from them, and when the bubbles touch her skin, they tickle!

Pickles smiles and wishes she had pickles to offer the glow worms for their tickles.

She hears a strange noise, and an old octopus drifts over to her from across the cave.

Pickles jumps!

"Don't be afraid," the octopus murmurs. "Why are you crying?"

"Oh, um ... " Pickles takes a deep breath. "There's a mermaid named Rainy who doesn't like me. She makes fun of my name."

The octopus understands. "Does it hurt?"

"Does it hurt?" Pickles repeats, confused. **"Well, on the inside, it hurts my feelings."**

The octopus smiles. "Do you have friends, Pickles?"

"Lots!" Pickles exclaims. "We play together and have fun!"

"And how do you feel then?" the octopus asks.

Pickles laughs and says, "I feel warm and happy!"

The octopus nods. "When Rainy is mean, you forget about your friends and think only about the bad feelings."

Pickles sighs. "Well, it's hard not to. Rainy always looks for me when I'm alone."

"*That is hard,*" the octopus agrees.
"Would it help to have a reminder? There is a special
conch shell. Whenever you're upset, make it sing."

Pickles holds out her hands. "Can I have it?"

"You must find it," the octopus explains.
"But once you do, you'll always remember that you
are loved just the way you are."

The octopus leads Pickles out of the cave. "Swim through the kelp forest and seek guidance from the sea creatures you meet."

Pickles looks at the forest. "I am brave." She gulps.
She swims towards the huge kelp fronds, and as they wave
back and forth, she whispers, "Oh, I don't like this."

Suddenly, a sea otter bumps into her.
"Sorry! I'm Ollie. Who are you?"

"I'm Pickles, and I'm looking for a singing conch shell."

"I think I know where it is," replies Ollie.
"But it's far away and **REALLY** deep down."

Pickles takes a shaky breath then asks, "Can you show me?"

"I can only go part way."

Pickles follows Ollie until it is very dark and gloomy. She looks around, but Ollie is gone.

Pickles begins to worry.

"Don't cry, Pickles."

Pickles peers into the dark and notices a faint shimmer. "Who are you?"

A starfish floats closer.

"I'm Twinkle. Are you looking for a special singing conch shell?"

Pickles nods.

"We can guide you there," Twinkle says.
"But it's dangerous."

Beneath her, dozens of starfish line up.
They shine like the stars in the sky!

"I can't stop searching now. I've come too far!"

The starfish form a path for Pickles,
so she follows them along the ocean floor.

Pickles discovers a beautiful coral garden.
"There! That's it—the conch shell!"
She points behind a luminous sea anemone
to a seashell on a bed of seagrass.
Pickles turns to thank the starfish,
but they are gone.

Just as she reaches for the shell,
a **HUGE SHARK** darts out from behind the coral!
His mouth opens wide and his teeth gleam.

"WHO ARE YOU?" he bellows.

"I-I'm Pickles," she stammers,
her voice shaky.

"Pickles? What kind of silly name is that?"

"It's not silly! It's ... " Pickles pauses.
"Hey! You're just like Rainy. You're mean!"

"I am not! Well, maybe a bit," the shark admits.
"Everyone is afraid to be my friend."

"Does it hurt?" Pickles asks.

"*Does it hurt?*" the shark asks uncertainly.
"Well ... on the inside it hurts. It hurts my feelings."

Pickles stares at the shark.
"I have an idea," she says. "Can you let me
have that shell?"

"Nope. It's a very special shell.
I don't know why, but it is."

"I know why," Pickles declares. "I can show you."
She swims past the shark and into the coral garden.

"You're brave," he says.

Pickles smiles. "I am. I am brave!"
She picks up the shell and blows into it.

The music is magical!

"I remember this song," Pickles says.
"It's a lullaby my mom sang to me!"

"It's beautiful," agrees the shark, tearing up.
"Sorry. This is embarrassing."

"There, there," says Pickles. "Crying is good for us."

The shark sniffles, and Pickles blows into the shell again. She remembers how much she is loved by her family and friends.

Now it is time for Pickles to go home.

She gives the shark a tickle, they giggle and he promises not to be mean ever again.

Pickles swims and swims, and when she finally arrives home, her mermaid friends rush to greet her!

Pickles tells them all about her journey and blows into the special singing conch shell for them to hear.

Her friends are still as they listen in awe!

They all smile and dance!

Unexpectedly, Pickles sees Rainy.
Oh no, she thinks.

She grips the shell and remembers how
the music makes her feel warm and loved.
She doesn't want to run away and hide!

"Hello, Rainy," she says in a steady,
confident voice.

Rainy takes a deep breath.
"Hello, Pickles. I-I missed your giggles
and tickles ... "
She starts to swim away.

"Wait!" Pickles calls to her.

"Would you like to blow into the conch shell?"

Rainy smiles and takes the shell.

Again, the music is magical!

"ATTENTION!" Pickles calls out,
"I haven't had a pickle in days. Let's have a pickle party!"

Everyone shares tickles, giggles and eats **LOTS** of pickles!

About the Author

Laura is a retired educator, wife, mom, "Lola" and now author! Laura obtained her Masters of Education from the University of Cincinnati, and teaching for almost two decades set the stage for her latest project—publishing her debut children's book, *Pickles The Mermaid*. A recent move to the beautiful hills of Pennsboro, West Virginia from Cincinnati, Ohio (where she was born and raised) allows her more time in nature with her retired sled dogs, Mistral and Sila. She also finds inspiration in yoga, hiking, tennis and travel. She believes there is magic in this story, but her hope is for children and adults alike to remember that the true magic within all of us is to believe in ourselves!

You can learn more about Laura on her website at
www.laurastrachanbooks.com

About the Illustrator

Michelle Simpson has illustrated many children's books, including *The Dancing Trees, I Can See You*, and the Jordan and Max series. She has also worked as a background and concept artist for kids' cartoons, the most recent being *The Happy House of Frightenstein*. Michelle holds a BAA in illustration from Sheridan College and lives in Niagara Falls, Ontario. Some of her inspirations include nature, animals and mythical creatures.

Made in the USA
Columbia, SC
21 August 2024